IN PREPARATION FOR A STORY
AND OTHER STORIES

ALSO BY GRACIELA TREVISAN

Cattail Stories

IN PREPARATION FOR A STORY

AND OTHER STORIES

Graciela Trevisan

Cover art: *Bird-Figure-Landscape* by Anne Marguerite Herbst
www.anneherbst.com
Book and Cover Design by Yizhou Guo
Author photograph by Lisa Rofel

DEDICATED TO

Lisa and Greta Gracie
And Alejandro, in loving memory

Contents

Acknowledgements viii

In Preparation for a Story 1

Rehearsing 4

Alicia 14

Un hombre/el otoño 17

A Man/Autumn 21

A Questionable Memoir 25

Reflections of a Silver Tabby Cat 30

Looking for Safety 35

Juego de niños 38

Children's Play 42

The President's Nightmare 46

? Or Else 50

MM en el P de la E 53

"MM en el P de la E" 56

I Saw Her at the Corner of Page and Folsom Waiting for the Bus 59

Little Annie 64

Ute, the Silver Tabby Cat 66

Atardecer/anochecer – un dilema 72

Sunset/Twilight: A Dilemma 75

Canción infantil de ayer – con variaciones necesarias de hoy 78

Children's Spanish Round from the Past – With Some Necessary Variations from Today 81

Intermezzo 85

Intermezzo 87

An Occasional Meeting 89

Exiting Remarks 94

*All stories originally written in Spanish were translated into English by the author in 2022

ACKNOWLEDGEMENTS

With gratitude and many thanks to Lisa Rofel, Donna Haraway, Megan Moodie, Anne Marguerite Herbst, Eli Andrew Ramer, Marisa Busso and Nelly Vuksic.

I don't want to have the terrible limitation of the person who lives only by what can be made to make sense. Not I, no: what I want is an invented truth.

Clarice Lispector, *The Stream of Life*

4. Do you think that your book will be commercially profitable?

Without consulting the woman, Morris wrote: "As profitable as soap or as electric mixers; it depends on the methods of marketing."

Cristina Peri Rossi, *The Ship of Fools*

The poets were in search of words they didn't know as well as words they did know and had lost.

Eduardo Galeano, *The Book of Embraces*

In Preparation for a Story

Now – Tuesday morning,
I am confronted with a blank page. What to do about it?
Many possibilities. Write, write, and again write. Make a
drawing. Tear it apart. Make a paper boat with it. Write the
list for the grocery store. Make a ball and give it to my cat to
play with.

Write, write and again write.

What about if I can't write. What happens when I can't?
Where do the page and the pages go?

Pages start flying, go around the globe, go beyond our
solar system and penetrate into other galaxies, go to the end
of the universe. But what happens if the universe doesn't
have an end? They continue traveling, trying in vain to reach
the end. Maybe they want to reach the end of a story, not
the end of the universe. Being wise, the pages might know
the universe has no end.

(The end of a story: that could be more complicated than the end of the universe. In many cases I look to the end of a story, but the story, just like the universe, has no end either.)

I like stories with no end. Some people get irritated with stories that never end. Perhaps they don't want the stories to survive *them*. They finish and the stories continue, because they have no end. The stories reach the pages flying in the universe, and join the pages to form a kind of unity. Pages-stories. Assuming these stories are all for the pages. They are written stories. The other ones, the ones I say, you say, we say, orally... where do they go? Do they also fly beyond our solar system? Do they penetrate other galaxies? Do I get any answers to these questions?

There are many, an infinite number of questions that have no answers. Stories, pages, the universe, can have many answers, half-answers and none at all. Let the scientists, philosophers, scholars of all types, look for the answers. They have been looking for them for millennia.

Let's walk, or sit down, and imagine a story. Then, let's write it.

There was once... There was once... There was once...

Mystery is engulfing my Imagination. It doesn't let me open my Imagination. Mystery is like a guard at the door of my Imagination, and doesn't want me to get in. I am going to sit down and wait until he goes for lunch. Because he has to go for lunch at some point. Ha! I will be patient and wait. I will enter my Imagination when the guard is gone. Very soon, dear reader, dear listener. Very soon!

Waiting for Mystery to go for lunch

....

He went for lunch

....

He came back and told me he is leaving. He had a good lunch and he can leave me alone. Before walking away, he turned to me and told me there is no conflict between Mystery and Imagination. On the contrary, he said. And he repeated: On the contrary. Even when I am overprotective and guard the door to *your* Imagination.

Then......   can I proceed?

2020

Rehearsing

I am looking at a painting. Again, again and again. The painting you painted many years ago, mother. It's night with a full moon. It's unusually dark: the moon seems very high and there are drifting clouds. There is a house. The house has a window. Maybe there is another window but I don't see it from here. There is light inside the house. Or, there is light inside the room with the window. My first thought is, "how many watts does the light bulb have"? I am inclined to think "40", because 1) we always used low voltage light bulbs, 2) the painting is old, 3) the person in that house has to save electricity (like we used to do at home). Then, there is the question of who is in the house or who is in the room. (Does the house have one room only?) I have always come to the same conclusion here: there is one person: an old man sitting at the table under a single (40-watt) light bulb. The man is thinking. He is alone/he is old/he is not sad. I can add a cup of tea or coffee on the table. He is drinking tea or coffee. Most of the time he doesn't talk with anybody. His house stands alone near the road. No, this is my invention: I don't know if there is a road. There are trees and bushes surrounding his house and there is a path that goes, I can't see where. I can't say where because this house is in the middle of nowhere, in the middle of the imagination where there is no province and no country. I am not even sure there is a path from the house to someplace. Maybe there was one but not now. Maybe there is one now. Maybe the old man is thinking that after all these years he needs to make an effort and open a path.

I would like to sit at the table with the man. First, would he open the door for me? How would I get there? I can answer the last question easily: I have always been there, since I was six or seven. I have seen and thought about this painting a million times. The first question is more problematic. I have to use my imagination for the answer. Does he open the door to me? I need to spell out the question again: does he open the door to me? If he doesn't know me, he will. But I have the impression he does know me and is tired of my mental intrusions. In this case, I am not sure he will open the door. Since I am not sure but I want to be sitting at the table with him, I need to continue using my imagination. I knock at the door. He gets up, looks through the window, can't see anybody, and opens the door. He lets me in.

Now I am sitting at his table. It's a firm, solid, wooden table. He is sitting on one corner, I am sitting on the other.

He doesn't offer me tea or coffee. We talk: "your house, your life, yourself, the painting you are in, have always intrigued me," I say. He replies, "everything, including me, is your mother's imagination and creation." I knew that and I wonder if he is just saying it to say something or if he didn't know that I knew. I go on to talk about my mother. He listens with interest (or I think so). He must be interested. We are always interested in hearing about our creator(s). We want to know if our creator(s) think of us, care about us, is/are planning to make some changes or improvements to their creation. This man listens to me with interest. I tell him I never saw my mother trying to work on the painting again. I excuse her by saying she was always very busy. I don't tell him he is destined (or condemned?) to stay where he is, forever sitting at the table, with a cup of tea or coffee that will never empty, with a single 40-watt light bulb that will never burn, with trees and bushes surrounding his house, with or without a path. Forever night with a full moon, beautiful when it was just painted but faded now by drifting clouds. Forever in the house, in the night, in the painting, because my mother is gone.

I will stay sitting at his table a little longer, I decide. I feel a mixture of sympathy for and detachment from this old man. Sympathy because he is locked forever in the painting and his possibilities of movement are limited. Detachment because I can't see his face yet. He is not covering his face;

it's just that from here, writing and imagining the two of us in the painting/in his house, I cannot see his face. The "I" who is sitting at his table can obviously see his face since we are close to each other and, as I said, he is not covering it.

I am thinking the best thing I can do for him is to make him into a character. Then he can have more movement and flexibility if not freedom. I am not interested in his past and all the common questions we ask people: where are you from? – what do you do? – what's your marital status? I am interested in his here and now. But I also see that this here and now has to be created.

I tell him my intentions. He seems amused. "Make a character of an old man like me!", he says with a smile, "your mother put me in this painting but she didn't dare to show my face...". I interrupt him, "my mother would have never put in a painting somebody she was ashamed of. Besides, the purpose of her painting was the exterior, I mean, the creation of a certain mood by showing an almost dark landscape as a metaphor for loneliness." He raises his head and looks at me directly for the first time.

Words allow me to bring his face into view: I can see him now from here: slight bitterness in his lips, sad blue eyes, the passing of time marked all over him. He might be 85, but I am not good at guessing people's age. "You think I am 85 but

I am 89, your mother wanted it like that," he says, again looking at me directly. I have to admit it was easier when he did not look at me directly. He gets up, not without effort, and says, "I'll cooperate with you, that is, if you still want to make me into a character." I nod. "I'll start," he continues and moves to look for something in the only cabinet, "I'll prepare more coffee". (I finally know it's coffee he is drinking.) "The last time I went out, it was raining. That was three days ago. It might still be wet outside. I went out and walked a long distance to buy this coffee and some sugar. You might think the distance is not long because you have just come from there, but for an old man like me... besides from here the distance is longer... I also bought noodles and lentils. That was three days ago". Silence. "I like lentils. I don't eat a lot of meat because of my teeth." Silence. "This house, this house doesn't look like anything you could have imagined." "Let's not get into me," I say, "you are the character here." He continues, "many years ago, probably by the time your mother painted this painting, I had a bicycle and rode it to buy groceries and visit my friend." He stops and smiles, "but who is creating the character? *You* have to imagine me." I also smile, in part to hide my fear of writing, and I nod in agreement. From now on it's me who is going to talk. I say aloud and write, "your friend used to live ten minutes from here. You went to his house every Sunday afternoon. When it rained and the road was muddy, you wore the boots you still have, that are leaning on the wall in

8

that corner, and walked. The two of you played cards, had coffee and a sip of grappa. Sometimes you put the grappa into the coffee. After three or four hours, you came back home. You always kept your bicycle inside the house. That's why my mother didn't paint it. You came back home and sat at this table and smiled. It had been a good few hours of comradeship, entertainment, and fresh air, even when it rained. You looked forward to Sunday afternoon. However, seven years ago you stopped going to your friend's. I am not clear why. I could mention several possibilities but this is not the moment to waste time doing that. Since then, you spend Sunday afternoons right here, sitting at the table. Sometimes you pull out the cards and play solitaire. You can spend many hours playing solitaire. And not only on Sunday afternoons. Other times you open the cabinet and take a picture and bring it to the table. You sit and look at it. It's not a photograph. It's a drawing, a Chinese drawing of a landscape with a lake and trees. I don't know how you got it but you enjoy looking at it. It perhaps brings you memories of unknown places and times. It's understandable. We all do that. A few times you stand at the window and look out. There is not much out there but it's a distraction. I would add that you hope to see somebody passing by, but here in this location that's unlikely. However, once or twice you saw a person. The first time, a middle-aged woman passed by carrying a big bag, apparently heavy, and you wondered for hours about the content of the bag. The second time, a boy of about 12 (again, I am not good at guessing people's age) passed by and when he saw you at the window, behind the glass, he paused and waved his hand. You were surprised and didn't wave back at him. The boy left and you would have liked to see him again but he never returned. In this location, it's unlikely to see people passing by. But you like to look out from time to time. Sometimes it rains, sometimes it's sunny, it's cloudy, it's dark, it's night. It's night, you go to bed around 9:30. You sleep on your back. In your dreams there is always a big open field on a sunny day. (How do I dare to go that far, into his dreams, but he doesn't complain.) You hear voices: they are not distant but it's hard to say where they come from. Perhaps these dreams are memories of imagined places and times. Or perhaps they are not."

I continue, "many years ago, by the time my mother painted this painting, you made a path from your house to the road. Weeds kept closing your path until you gave up. 'No more weeding, let them grow', you said. Now I realize you opened a path a long time ago, it just didn't last. I would offer to help you pull out the weeds, but there is not enough time in a story like this one to spend three or four hours weeding a path... You know, soon it will be spring and this eternal night of the painting with the full moon might fade away. I don't even want to think of that possibility. It would mean losing the painting: I can't bear the thought of it. So let me retrieve those words and erase them: soon it will be spring and this eternal night of the painting with the full moon might fade away."

"I said I was interested in your now and here, but your past keeps coming and mixing with your present. And in this present you don't have many possessions. This table and three chairs. Who has sat at this table before me? (I keep interrogating your past, and you smile). There is a small stove: three burners and an oven. There is a cabinet which you opened a while ago to get the coffee, and I saw three plates, three glasses, three cups, a bowl, the noodles and lentils you mentioned earlier, a jar where I suppose you put the sugar and two small boxes which I don't know what they have. There is a board on a sawhorse next to the stove: I see a small knife, a piece of paper, a marmalade jar with nails, and an onion. You didn't buy that onion three days ago. That onion is old and I am not sure if you are planning to use it when you cook the lentils or the noodles. There is no refrigerator, which is understandable because this painting is very old. (When my mother painted it, she didn't have a refrigerator herself.). On the floor, next to the stove, two bottles: a red wine bottle, half-drunk, and a bottle with kerosene. On the floor, in the corner, far from the table, I see a kerosene lamp. In this remote location the electricity goes out frequently. Your eating pattern is erratic. You were just about to have a piece of cheese when I arrived. You keep it in the oven, along with a pan, a small pot and a half loaf of bread. Three days ago you went out and walked a long distance to buy noodles, lentils, coffee, sugar, cheese and bread. Maybe the bottle of red wine, now half-drunk. You don't have to offer me cheese and bread. I didn't come here to eat. I said, 'let's sit at the table with the man', you opened the door and here I am sitting in front of you. Trying to make a character of you. A character without a name... And as I write, nothing gets clear. I despair at missing this opportunity to know you, after so many years thinking of your existence, thinking you were here, where you are..."

I would like to know what my mother thinks of all this. Without consulting with her I came into his house, I met the old man. I have been curious about him all my life, and now I need my mother's help to continue. I don't know what to do with him, and how to get out of his house, his life, my story. Should I think of his name? If I name him, I might be able to get out and perhaps help him get out too. But, where will he go? How can I know if he will ever die?

His death is not something for me to decide. No. The old man of the painting is not going to die. Not in my story. His life might seem meaningless, but he lives. He sits at the table, thinks, drinks coffee, and plays solitaire. He sometimes looks through the window and sees the seasons. He goes out and buys a few things. He has a small portable radio and listens to the news, commentaries, and music. He does this usually in the evening. I told him I'll bring him batteries next time I come. (But when will I come back?)

He doesn't need to leave the house. This is his home, he feels safe in it. He doesn't need to leave the painting. He has been for many years in it. He feels safe in it.

I see the answer, mother: I don't have to do anything with him. Simply leave him where he is and let him be. This will also be my way to get out. And the name? A name to place him into the world and my story? He knows his name: that's what matters. Not the name I can invent for him in this story.

I get up and say goodbye to him. We shake hands and I leave. The night is cold, the full moon seems very high and it's faded by drifting clouds. It's dark, as it was in the beginning. I button my coat, put my pen in one pocket, my notebook under my arm, and walk away.

1991

Alicia

I shut the door and went to talk to Alicia. She said no no by no means. I told her it was stormy, it will probably rain, Celina will get wet, will get a cold. Alicia said I will not share my bed with anybody else. I felt disappointed. She is usually sensitive, and politically sensitive too, caring about causes and things like that. This time, however, she was hard, I won't share my bed anymore! You and your animals! I softly pointed out Celina was not *my* animal. But, yes, Alicia had to sleep with Micha, my cat born in my parents' house who wouldn't sleep on my bed but on hers. Alicia had to share her bed with Teresa, a one-year-old elephant who wanted to sleep under three blankets and I only had two. I admitted (and still do) all the inconveniences my friends caused her, including that evening I came home with Poli, my grandmother's parrot, who slept on my bed but kept talking loudly the whole night and Alicia couldn't sleep. I've always thought of you as a very sensitive woman Alicia, that's one of the reasons why we are roommates, because we both care about people, things, life and animals. Besides, needless to say, Celina is female and she has such a pretty name. Come and see her, she is sweet, very tall, that has nothing to do with sweetness I know, but she smiles, I love her smile... Alicia was sitting at the kitchen table and gave in a little: alright, but she has to sleep on your bed. How can I do that if Marta and Silvia share my bed! (Marta and Silvia: the two orphan lionesses I met at the bus station and brought home to live with us.) I couldn't believe Alicia's attitude. Celina was outside waiting in the cold, she just needed a place for one night, that was all, she was not staying in town, she didn't like big towns, and was on her way to the desert. From one desert to another, because she had spent most of her life in deserts. Such a privileged life, I thought. Alicia and I hadn't spent our lives in deserts. We both came from small towns and luckily for Celina we were in the city now because, at least in my hometown, they would not have accepted anybody like her. People are sometimes very narrow-minded and I was sorry because Alicia was acting like that, too. I tried one more thing to persuade her. She had prepared vegetable soup for dinner. I took my bowl full of soup and said, I will give this to Celina, I am not having dinner tonight. I saw tears coming out of her eyes, I don't mean to be cruel but it's too much, she said. I hugged her, we hugged each other and I cried with happiness when I heard her saying, tell Celina to come in, I will share my bed and my three blankets with her. Alicia is a wonderful woman, I thought. I went smiling to open the front door, come in Celina, please feel at home.

And as she was walking in, I realized, for the first time in my life, how beautiful, how elegant female dinosaurs are.

1981

Un hombre/el otoño

Érase un hombre que se enamoró del otoño. Parece que el metejón le había empezado de niño, cuando tenía nueve años, según él mismo lo reveló en un diario que escribía y escribe desde hace mucho tiempo. Dice en el diario que una tarde de domingo, después del almuerzo, y cuando todos dormían la siesta, se fue a caminar por el boulevard donde termina su pueblo y empieza el campo, es decir, el campo propiamente dicho. Los árboles, esos árboles altos que, dice en su diario, nunca estuvo seguro cómo se llamaban, estaban llenos de hojas marrones, muchas ya caídas al suelo. Esto ya lo había visto antes, por supuesto, después de todo tenía nueve años. Pero ese domingo a la tarde, a la hora de la siesta, sintió algo distinto, y se sintió distinto. Una calidez de voces anaranjadas y una luz color ladrillo, así dice que lo pensó en ese momento, lo hicieron parar y mirar a todos lados. Entonces lo vio, jura que vio el otoño. Aclara de que no era una persona, o un hombre, o una figura transparente. No, eso sería demasiado literal, digo yo, la narradora. Él aclara de que no sabe lo que era, pero algo que lo envolvió y absorbió, como si hubiera sido infatuado por ese algo, mezcla de colores, sonidos pequeños, olores, un Tiempo infinito y transparente que lo hizo aspirar y aspirar y mirar hacia arriba.

Eso fue a los nueve años, hace mucho ya. Pero desde entonces, ha estado enamorado del otoño. Los días han pasado, y también los años, y él ha seguido enamorado. De niño y adolescente, siempre esperando que llegara el otoño. Después, más tarde, también esperándolo. Y siempre esperándolo.

Hasta que se convirtió en hombre grande, como se dice, o también se dice, hombre maduro. Y este hombre grande o maduro decidió buscarlo, seguirlo, vivir con el otoño donde sea que se encuentre, donde sea que viaje. En otras palabras, al amor hay que vivirlo. Y él se propuso vivirlo, y vivir con su amor. Le escribe poemas, que no publica para que nadie sepa de la seriedad de su amor (después de todo tantos poetas y tantas poetisas le han escrito al otoño, pero eso es diferente, piensa, y él no es celoso).

Ya hace bastante que viaja. Viaja adonde se encuentre el otoño, su compañero del alma, para repetir el término de Miguel Hernández en uno de sus poemas, y que todos y todas usamos. Viaja con una valija pequeña, porque no necesita mucho con el otoño, no hace frío intenso y no lleva sobretodo ni bufanda ni gorro. Viaja, y la gente de distintos lugares le dice que el otoño no es el mismo en todas partes, pero él les dice que sí, que es el mismo, que lo sabe porque ha viajado mucho y lo ha visto y estado con él. Hay gente que le dice "aquí hay flores amarillas en el otoño" y él les contesta que en su pueblo natal también hay flores amarillas en el otoño. Hay mujeres que le dicen que la brisa y el sol otoñal (según él, así los llaman, brisa y sol otoñal) les permite secar la ropa al aire libre con más facilidad, y él agrega que en su pueblo natal su madre también secaba la ropa al aire libre con más facilidad por la brisa y el sol otoñal, y que en otros pueblos donde ha estado vio lo mismo. Hay hombres que le dicen que es lindo sentarse a la puerta en el otoño porque no hace frío ni calor, y él les dice que ha visto mucha gente hacer lo mismo cuando el otoño está en otros pueblos, en otras regiones. Pero cuando les habla de las voces anaranjadas, ah! eso no, no han escuchado las voces anaranjadas del otoño. Entonces sabe de que éste es su secreto, ésta es la intimidad que comparte con el otoño, y que es única a él, y en todas partes con él.

Por regla, cuando viaja en busca de su compañero del alma, no dice que está enamorado, que vive enamorado, no sea que le quiten la intimidad, no sea que en ese pueblo o región castiguen o destierren a quien ama algo o a alguien que, gramaticalmente hablando, es de su mismo género. Sólo se lo confió a una nenita que en uno de sus viajes le preguntó por qué viajaba tanto y él le respondió "para seguir al otoño". La nenita, de nombre Yazmín, le preguntó si estaba enamorado del otoño y contestó que sí, que lo estaba. Ella no pareció sorprenderse y dijo que ella también, que ella también estaba enamorada del otoño. Pero Yazmín es una nenita, sólo una nenita que no puede viajar, por ahora, pensó él.

Érase un hombre: este nuestro hombre de esta historia, con su valija pequeña y su diario a cuestas, continúa sus viajes. Digo "érase" porque por alguna razón que escapa a mi entendimiento, este hombre viaja y viajará siempre, por los siglos de los siglos, como si perteneciera a uno de esos cuentos de antes que empezaban con "érase". Dicen que el amor dura más allá de no sé qué, de la muerte, creo que dicen. También dicen por allí que la muerte es vencida por el amor, o que el amor vence a la muerte, lo cual es lo mismo. Sea como sea, nuestro hombre continúa sus viajes siguiendo al otoño. Y el otoño no es indiferente, lo espera, lo acaricia, le habla (supongo que a su manera, en la lengua del otoño), le hace el amor, lo duerme, y hasta le cuenta cuentos. ¡Qué ocurrencia! ¡le cuenta cuentos! Me encantaría escuchar uno de los cuentos, porque no puedo imaginarme qué cuentos el otoño le contará al hombre enamorado del otoño.

2016

A Man/Autumn

There was once a man who fell in love with Autumn. It seems that the infatuation started when he was a child, when he was nine years old, according to his own admission in a diary that he began to write a long time ago and continues to write. He says in his diary that on a Sunday early afternoon, after lunch, and when everybody was taking the siesta, he went to walk by the boulevard where the town ends and the country starts, that is to say, the country properly speaking. The trees, those tall trees that he says in his diary he was never sure what they were called, were full of brown leaves, many of them already fallen to the ground. He had already seen this before, of course, after all he was nine years old. But that Sunday early afternoon, at siesta time, it felt different and he felt different. A warm sensation of orange voices and a light the color of brick, that's what he thought at that moment, he says, forced him to stop and look everywhere. Then, he saw it, he swears he saw the Autumn. He clarifies it was not a person, or a man, or a transparent figure. No, that would be too literal, I, the narrator, say. He stresses he didn't know what it was, but something wrapped around him and absorbed him, as if he were infatuated by *that* something, a mix of colors, small sounds, smells, and an infinite and transparent Time that made him breathe, breathe, and look up.

That was when he was nine, a long time ago, long time ago. But since then, he has been in love with Autumn. Days have passed, the years too, and he has continued being in love. As a child and a teenager, he was always waiting for Autumn's arrival. After, later, he also waited for it. Always waiting for it.

Until he became a big man, as they say, or they also say, a mature man. And this big man or mature man, decided to look for the Autumn, to follow it, to live with it wherever it was, wherever it traveled. In other words, love must be lived. And he was determined to live it, and to live with his love. He writes poems, which he doesn't publish so nobody will know the seriousness of his love (after all, so many poets have written to Autumn, but that's different, he thinks, and he is not jealous).

He has been traveling for quite a while. He travels wherever Autumn is, "his soulmate", to repeat the term of Miguel Hernández in one his poems, a term we all use. He travels with a small suitcase, because he doesn't need much with Autumn, it's not too cold, and he doesn't carry an overcoat or a scarf or a hat. He travels, and people from different places tell him that Autumn is not the same everywhere. But he tells them Yes, it is the same, he knows because he has traveled a lot and he has seen it and been with it. People tell him there are yellow wild flowers here in Autumn and he answers that in his hometown there are also yellow wild flowers in Autumn. There are women who tell him the Autumnal breeze and sun (according to him, they say it like that, Autumnal breeze and sun) allow them to dry clothes outdoors more easily, and he says that in his hometown his mother also used to dry clothes outdoors more easily because of the Autumnal breeze and sun, and he adds that he also saw this in other towns where he has been. There are men who tell him that it's nice to sit by the front door in Autumn because it's neither cold nor hot, and he says that he has seen many people do the same when Autumn is in other towns, in other regions. But when he mentions the orange voices, Ah! No, No! They have not heard the orange voices of Autumn. Then he knows that this is his secret, this is the intimacy he shares with Autumn, and it's unique to him, and everywhere with him.

As a rule, when he travels in search of his soulmate, he doesn't say that he is in love, that he lives in love, lest they take away his intimacy, lest in that town or region they punish or banish the one who is in love with something or someone who is not clearly from the opposite sex, or who is, grammatically speaking, of the same sex. He entrusted it only to a little girl who on one of his trips asked him why he traveled so much and he replied to follow Autumn. The little girl, whose name was Yazmín, asked him if he was in love with Autumn, and he answered Yes, he was. She didn't seem to be surprised and said that she too, she too was in love with Autumn. But Yasmín is a little girl, only a little girl who cannot travel right now, he thought.

There was once a man: our man of this story, with his small suitcase and his diary, traveling and traveling. I say "there was once a man" because for some reason beyond my understanding, this man travels and will travel forever and ever, down through the centuries, as if he belongs to one of those tales from before, that began "there was once..." or something like that. They say that love lasts beyond I don't know what, beyond death, I think they say. They also say that death is defeated by love, or that love defeats death, which is the same thing. Be that as it may, our man continues his travels following Autumn. And Autumn is not indifferent, it waits for him, caresses him, speaks to him (I guess in its own way, in the language of Autumn), makes love to him, puts him to sleep and even tells him stories. What an idea! It tells him stories! I would love to listen to one of them, because I cannot imagine what stories Autumn might tell to the man in love with the Autumn.

2022

A Questionable Memoir

Why did Cecilia want to go rescue parrots in Patagonia?

Suppose she was tired of buying honey, jars and jars of honey. She got tired of being the honey caretaker. And she got tired of being harassed by the mailman and the police for having too many jars of honey at home. Another reason: she couldn't stand our condescending attitude. Susana and I would go out of our way to ease her work as the honey caretaker. Cecilia was a grown-up, mature woman who couldn't stand paternalistic attitudes reflected, as she thought, in our support. I can also imagine she perhaps felt her life was dull: cafés, political meetings, office work, cafés again, more political meetings, rallies, discussions, and a lot of rain that winter. On the positive side, she loved birds, all kinds of birds, and told me that she had read parrots were in danger in Patagonia, particularly parrots who didn't talk or talked very little, and needed to be rescued.

She left on a Sunday morning. I thought Sundays were nostalgic enough without having to see her depart. Empty room, empty shelves (with a few jars of honey left), empty hearts, those of Susana and me. Despite that we heard her explanation why she had to leave us, for many days we continued asking the same question (sometimes to ourselves, sometimes aloud to whoever wanted to hear it):

Why did Cecilia leave us to go rescue parrots in Patagonia?

Maybe she was unhappy with me, guilty of not being the political activist she would have liked me to be. In the same vein, she might have also been unhappy with Susana, who was too busy finishing her university degree and singing the national anthem at schools and in front of the mirror in the old building's lobby where we lived. However, to our credit, we ate honey every day, several times a day, particularly if Cecilia was around. If she was around for lunch, if the three of us were around for lunch, a jar of honey was invariably brought to the table. Cecilia put honey in her salad and wanted us to do the same. Not having a very sophisticated taste, I refused to do so, and this provoked some friction between us. Susana, very stoically, put honey in her salad, and I could see her struggle to mix the honey with the lettuce, tomatoes and scallions. She did it though. Honey into the mashed potatoes: I could tolerate it, honey with roasted potatoes, honey with noodles, honey with beets... but not in my lettuce-tomato-scallion salad. This was a reason for friction between us, as was the fact that she insisted I put moisture on my face by using honey every night before going to bed. No, Cecilia, I couldn't go that far.

Living with roommates when you are a student and have little or no money could be a reason for friendship and camaraderie, adding the fact that our politics were quite similar. The three of us had been roommates for a while, and we remained so despite the big change experienced when Cecilia said, "we all need to eat more honey," and started to bring jars and more jars of honey home. Our apartment wasn't big enough to accommodate so many jars of honey, and we had to put some under our beds, inside the oven, and on a window that faced an internal courtyard. We were on the 5th floor, and the courtyard or little patio belonged to the 1st floor. When one morning Susana inadvertently closed the window (we held it open because of the jars of honey) and three jars fell and crashed onto the patio of the 1st floor, the neighbors reported us to the police, and the police came suspecting we were hiding something. We let them see all the honey we had, and they looked at us confused and asked us if honey played some role in the revolution we wanted to make (just because of the fact we were students, the police assumed we wanted to make a revolution.) The person delivering the mail also left us a note complaining about the two jars of honey in our mailbox. We politely told him he could take a jar for his family, but we necessarily needed to use the mailbox because we didn't have enough space to put all the jars in our apartment. He took a jar of honey, and later another one, and never complained again. But once again I was confronted with the question:

Why did Cecilia leave us to go rescue parrots in Patagonia?

Susana graduated on a rainy day, at the end of spring. She needed to find a job, and found one at a university in the north of the country. I moved out from the apartment because, without her, I couldn't afford the rent by myself. By then, all the honey was gone, long gone, as was Cecilia. However, I remember when I was about to close the door before leaving for the last time: I looked back at the living room and saw hundreds of jars of honey on the floor. I said aloud, "Cecilia, are you planning to come back?" I heard no answer. I closed the door and went to the elevator. But I couldn't help it: I took a piece of paper and pen from my bag, wrote on it

Why did Cecilia leave us to go rescue parrots in Patagonia?

and posted it on the elevator door. When I got to the first floor, somebody was waiting to go up, looked at the piece of paper, read it, and made a face. I told him that I had posted it, and went out to the busy street. By then, night had fallen.

2015

Reflections of a Silver Tabby Cat

For Ute

Since I heard my moms talking about compassion, I have been pondering it. What is it? Am I compassionate? How can I become a compassionate being?

Most of my life I have been wandering in the house and garden, eating well and sleeping.

I like to sit in the garden when the sun is there. I feel warm and happy. I see the blue jays coming and going, and I like them. I let them be. I must admit that when I was much younger I was in the hunter mood, and tried to get a blue jay when she flew and perched on a branch. Don't worry: I was never able to do it. Now, I look at them and say hello, because my moms also say hello to them.

Occasionally I play with one of my moms in the bedroom, or I watch *her* play with little balls. I know she tries to entertain me.

I like to be petted and petted for a long time, and often. In this, I am demanding.

When one of my moms is petting me, she says a lot of good things to me. She says that I am a good girl, a sweet girl, a brave girl, a smart girl, an enduring girl, a stoic girl, a teacher girl, and a wonderful girl. She tells me all that! I feel so good, what can I say!

I have had several health problems, and I had two surgeries, at different times and for different issues. It was awful, very traumatic, but I recovered well thanks to the doctors and my moms.

I still have health problems: asthma, allergies. They make me sneeze a lot! And I have hyperthyroidism (difficult word for me!), and my moms have to give me medicine every day to keep my thyroid level normal.

As I was saying, I spend quite a bit of time in the garden. There are two cats from a neighbor's home who I really dislike, and I dislike them a lot when they come to my garden.

This takes me to think about compassion. Should I be patient with them? Should I be tolerant of them? Should I tell them, "let me bring you some food," or "you can share my garden for a while"?

But this last thing is so hard for me! I do not want to share *my* garden with them, or with any other cat. Am I being too territorial, possessive, selfish?

If I am not territorial, possessive and selfish, would I then be compassionate? Will sharing my space in a friendly and understanding manner make me compassionate? What do you think? And, does being compassionate end there?

I guess this would be a beginning. And then, what about what happens outside my garden? I hear my moms talking about what is going on in the world. Between my meals, the garden, grooming myself and sleeping, I also have time to think about the world.

How can I be compassionate with all sentient beings of all species, particularly those more in need? I heard my moms saying it's important to be *actively* compassionate. Active compassion, aha! Well, if I offer my neighboring cats some food or I invite them to stay in my garden for a while, that *is* active compassion.

But how to exercise it towards all sentient beings of all species in the world?

My freedom is limited and they don't let me go beyond the garden. Maybe I should be happy with small acts of active compassion, towards the cats who come to my garden, towards my moms, towards their friends, relatives and neighbors who occasionally come to visit.

By the way, I should encourage all the human visitors to pet me.

I will also say a purring prayer for all sentient beings of all species in the world who need help, who are lonely, who are marginalized and who are oppressed.

And my prayer will be loud, very feline and full of love! and will travel and reach them wherever they are!

I will fill them with my good energy and my love!

You will hear my meow across oceans and continents! It will be so loud and loving that my moms will say to me, "you are one of a kind, sweetie, but that's a bit too loud!"

For now, those will be my acts of active compassion. I need to use my imagination to create more of them.

I leave a blank below for you, readers of all species, genders, sizes, ages, abilities and colors, to draw any suggestions you want. A big meow to you all!

2018

Looking for Safety

Looking for safety I went into the label of the tin box. "A blend of Ceylon and India tea," a woman's voice told me from the label. I said, "Fine, I like tea." But I hadn't come looking for a cup of tea. I had come looking for safety. The young lady on the label offered me a chair and some tea. She was having tea (a blend of Ceylon and India tea) sitting at the window, enjoying the view of her family's immense garden in the Fall. I sat in front of her, at the small table where the teapot, the cups and saucers were. "Do you take milk?" she asked me, in her perfect British accent. "No," I said, "only some sugar." My English wasn't perfect and she noticed it. She looked at me, and just when I was afraid she would ask me to leave, she said in her sweet and commanding tone, "You are not British, are you"? "No, I am not. I am sorry" I replied, "can I stay, anyway"? "Yes, you can, so long as you pronounce the 'w' correctly, and do not forget to pronounce the 's' at the end of a word." Those were her last words for a long time. She looked through the window, sad but content, and I realized she was far away. "What is she thinking"? I wondered. I felt quite safe, and entertained myself imagining her thoughts. She is thinking about the last book of poetry she has read… She is thinking about the love poem her fiancé wrote to her… I don't know if she has a fiancé but she must, otherwise she wouldn't be so calm and safe on the label of this box. Perhaps she would have preferred to have *him* sitting in this chair. Instead, here I am, in my pursuit of safety, I have taken the chair reserved for him. "Would you like some more tea"? she asked me, after several hours of silence and an empty cup. I wanted to give her the exact answer, the perfect British answer, but I wasn't sure and said, "I would like some more tea" simply repeating her words. She looked at me again and poured tea into my cup. We continued in silence for several more hours. During those hours, she looked through the window and I realized she was far away. I looked through the window too, and felt nostalgic for a stable and safe world. I felt envious of her for having so much, and so much safety. As if reading my thoughts (but she wasn't because she was far away), she looked at me again (this was the third time) and began to talk, "I have been on this box's label for more than a century. I love the garden, the Fall, the tea, the tranquility and safety of an uneventful life. But I want to try the world, the land where you come from. Can we switch places for a year or two"? I accepted the change. I didn't want her fiancé, but I wanted her chair, the table, the teapot, the cups, the window, the garden, and the blend of Ceylon and India tea. It was a good arrangement. I don't know where she is now, but I am here sitting at her table, drinking tea, looking through the window, feeling melancholic but safe. I am the woman you see on the box's label when you buy this fine blend of Ceylon and India tea. But I must admit my British-English is still not perfect, my "w" is not good enough, and my "s" sometimes does not come out from my mouth at the end of a word.

2001

Juego de niños

A R. por supuesto

Cuando tenía siete años y mi primo Rodolfo cinco
solíamos salir al atardecer, después de tanto pan y manteca
dos más dos son cuatro y mamá por lo menos veinte veces
con que nuestra abuela común nos mantenía desde la siesta
hasta las seis. Solíamos salir y nos íbamos lejos, a las afueras
del pueblo, que no era grande pero exigía caminar varias
cuadras para salir de él. Allí nos sentábamos en el cesped a
esperar que cayeran los rayos de sol. Habíamos calculado,
después de algunas observaciones directas, que los rayos
empezaban a caer cuando el sol empezaba a inclinarse para
irse. Controlada con un reloj, que le había sacado a mi papá
sin que se diera cuenta, la caída ocurría alrededor de las
siete, en ese tiempo de primavera tan lindo en que al cesped
le crecían florcitas amarillas con un perfume muy fresco y
suave. Rodolfo llevaba siempre una cacerola vieja que a
pesar de su vejez conservaba la tapa intacta, lo cual era
necesario para encerrar los rayos. Yo había conseguido un
tarro tamaño mediano de masitas Canale que mi mamá
usaba para guardar las arvejas. A pesar de ellas, mamá había

accedido sin demasiadas preguntas a dármelo, creyendo que el tarro sería utilizado para poner los huevos de caracol que en un tiempo anterior a los rayos solíamos recoger.

Por falta de práctica, en los primeros días nos resultó difícil agarrar los rayos de sol. Perdimos algunos muy lindos. Marta, nuestra prima, que también andaba en esta actividad con su barra aunque en distinto sitio de las afueras del pueblo, nos había advertido del peligro de quemarnos los dedos. La cuestión era agarrarlos suavemente con el índice y el pulgar, con cuidado de no quebrarlos. Nuestra torpeza, fruto de la inexperiencia, nos llevó a romper varios que hubieran sido nuestro orgullo ante Marta y su barra, sin contar que tuvimos que planear un robo al botiquín de primeros auxilios de la abuela y sacar cierta cantidad de Curitas para cubrir una que otra marca de quemadura y en previsión de futuros accidentes. Rodolfo lloró el tercer día, tan llorón como siempre, y yo estuve a punto de plantar bandera y decir "muy bien no venimos más". Pero al día siguiente, convencidos que a pesar de los fracasos, volvimos al mismo sitio: él con su cacerola vieja, yo con mi lata de masitas Canale.

Desde entonces todo anduvo sobre ruedas. Los rayos caían amarillos rojos verdes anaranjados algunos grises un poco tristes blancos imposibles distinguirlos. La cacerola y el tarro se iban llenando poco a poco de rayos de sol. Poco a poco porque en realidad nunca terminaban de llenarse: hecho completamente explicable teniendo en cuento lo delgado que eran los rayos. Absolutamente delgados y transparentes. En esas tardes de caída de rayos de sol nosotros éramos felices. Corríamos y nos tirábamos al suelo abarajándolos. Nos reíamos cuando se nos rompía alguno. No nos importaba nada: todo era los rayos de sol y nosotros. En esos días de primavera.

Pero el tiempo vino y vino demasiado pronto: a las dos semanas cuando mi mamá se dio cuenta que yo no guardaba huevos de caracol en la lata. El tiempo llegó cuando la mamá de Rodolfo dudó que la cacerola vieja fuera usada para hornear tortas de barro. Las madres hablaron entre ellas consultaron con sus maridos advirtieron a la abuela y al final los cinco, reunidos en asamblea familiar, nos preguntaron en qué andábamos. Mi primer impulso fue inventar cualquier cosa porque sabía que si decíamos la verdad iban a pensar que mentíamos. Pero Rodolfo, tan ingenuo como siempre, les dijo que juntábamos rayos de sol. No nos creyeron. Les dijimos que juntábamos rayos de sol y estaban en la cacerola vieja bien tapada y en la lata bien tapada de masitas Canale. No nos creyeron. Les dijimos que no se los podíamos mostrar porque si abríamos los recipientes los rayos se escaparían. No nos creyeron. Les dijimos que sí que era verdad allá en las afueras del pueblo corriendo por el cesped con florcitas de primavera amarillas y frescas. No nos creyeron.

Cuando abrieron el tarro de masitas Canale y los rayos de sol empezaron a salir, Rodolfo lloró. Yo en un acto desesperado me tiré sobre la cacerola vieja para salvar los que quedaban. Pero ellos me la quitaron la abrieron y dijeron a gritos "NO-VEN-QUE-NO-HAY-NADA". Rodolfo y yo veíamos cómo los rayos de sol se iban, desaparecían en el techo, en la habitación de al lado, se escapaban al patio por la puerta abierta. Pero ellos, ocupados en demostrar nuestra ingenuidad, no los veían. Y no los ven, cuando en las tardes de primavera, en las afueras del pueblo, los chicos corren sobre el cesped entre florcitas amarillas y frescas juntando rayos de sol en una cacerola vieja y en un tarro de masitas Canale.

1976

Children's Play

When I was seven years old and my cousin Rodolfo was five, we used to go out in the early evening, after lots of bread and butter two plus two is four and writing mamá at least twenty times with which our common grandma kept us from the siesta until six. We used to go out and we went far, to the outskirts of town, that was not very big but demanded walking several blocks. There we sat on the grass waiting for the rays of the sun to fall. We had calculated, after some direct observations, that the rays started to fall when the sun inclined to leave. Timing it with a watch, which I had taken from my dad without him noticing, the fall happened around seven, in that nice spring time when the grass grew little yellow flowers with a soft and fresh smell. Rodolfo always carried with him an old pot that despite its old age kept the lid intact, which was necessary to capture the rays. I had gotten a medium-sized can of Canale cookies that my mom used to store the peas. Despite the peas, mom had agreed without too many questions to give it to me, believing that the can would be used to put the snail eggs in that we used to collect in a time before the rays.

Due to lack of practice, in the first days it was difficult for us to catch the sun's rays. We lost some very nice ones. Marta, our cousin, who was doing the same thing with her friends but in a different part of the town's outskirts, had warned us of the risk of burning our fingers. The point was to grab them very gently with our thumb and forefinger, being careful not to break them. Our clumsiness, the result of inexperience, led us to break several that would have made us proud before Marta and her friends, not to mention that we had to plan a robbery of grandma's first aid kit to take out a certain number of Band-Aids to cover one after another burn mark and in anticipation of future incidents. Rodolfo cried on the third day, as he usually did, and I was about to "plant a flag" and say, "very well, we won't come anymore." But the next day, convinced despite the failures, we returned to the same place: he with his old pot, I with my can of Canale cookies.

After that, everything went smoothly. The rays fell yellow red green orange some grey a little sad white impossible to distinguish them. The pot and the can were little by little filling up with rays of sunlight. Little by little because in reality the pot and can never finished filling up: a completely explainable fact considering how thin the rays are. Absolutely thin and transparent. In those early evenings with the sun's rays falling we were happy. We ran and threw ourselves on the ground grabbing them. We laughed when a few broke. We didn't care about anything: everything was the rays of the sun and us. In those spring days.

But the time came and came too soon: two weeks later when my mom realized I wasn't putting snail eggs in the can. Time came when Rodolfo's mom doubted that the old pot was used to bake mud cakes. Our mothers talked between themselves consulted with their husbands warned grandma and in the end the five of them, gathered in a family assembly, asked us what we were up to. My first impulse was to invent whatever because I knew that if we told the truth they would think we were lying. But Rodolfo, as naïve as ever, told them we were gathering rays of the sun. They didn't believe us. We said we were gathering the sun's rays and they were in the old pot very well covered and in the very well-covered can of Canale cookies. They didn't believe us. We told them we couldn't show them because if we opened the containers the rays would escape. They didn't believe us. We said that Yes, it was true, there in the outskirts of town running on the grass with fresh, little yellow spring flowers. They didn't believe us.

When they opened the Canale cookies can and the rays started to come out, Rodolfo cried. In a desperate act, I threw myself on the old pot to save the ones left. But they took it away from me opened it and shouted "DON'T YOU

SEE THAT THERE IS NOTHING IN HERE." Rodolfo and I saw how the rays were leaving, disappearing into the ceiling, into the next room, escaping to the backyard through the open door. But they, busy in showing us our naiveté, did not see them. And they don't see them, when on early spring evenings, in the outskirts of town, children run on the grass among little fresh yellow flowers gathering the sun's rays in an old pot and in a can of Canale cookies.

2022

The President's Nightmare

The president of the republic, general commander of the armed forces, and president of the military junta, who holds three positions at the same time, has had a nightmare. This has been so vivid, so real that he has to do something. He thought of telling it to his wife. But the nightmare has been so vivid, so real that he cannot trust his wife, not even his 89-year-old mother. He cannot trust any woman at all, not even the babies inside their mothers' wombs who are going to be born females. The general has to do something and before dawn he is already sitting at his presidential desk in his presidential palace signing his latest presidential decree. Su excelencia sir president has just decreed that every woman in his country be interrogated. What for? the lieutenant-assistant asks, particularly concerned with the difficulty of such a task since women constitute more than half of the population. And the general says, we have to lock-up some women in this country. His assistant tries to understand the vagueness of the president's statement and so do the other members of the junta. They don't get the point though. Why "some women"? And how many of them? Is it that sir president wants to even-up the female with the male population? But the general has had the nightmare and he knows better than anybody else. In the evening he gives a short speech on the government-controlled television networks explaining to his people the need and usefulness of such a decree. It isn't meant to harass women, quite the contrary, it is meant to protect them. Because he, the other generals, and the whole army respect women very much and respect is basic to a christian nation and they are all good christians and women are meant to be mothers and queens of their homes as fathers are the bosses who bring food to the family and because the family is so dear to all generals, and because of this and because of that, women must be interrogated. How? the sergeant, who was in charge of torturing political prisoners for 15 years and has now been appointed as president of the supreme court, asks. How? he asks to the committee of 12 male psychologists, sociologists and lawyers in charge of preparing the interrogation. The answer is difficult, because as everyone knows, nobody knows the purpose of the presidential decree. However, the president is impatient, do not ask more questions, just do your job, he says to the committee, and looking at his fellow generals he adds, there are women in this country who are betrayers of our cause. A long silence follows this statement. Then one of the junta's members dares to ask, why don't you share your concerns with us? But the president really feels ashamed of his dream and of his fears. He doesn't want to describe his nightmare but at a meeting of the high command he assures them that some women, he doesn't know exactly how many, but some women are planning an insurrection to take over the government, which means that not only he but all of them will lose their lands and businesses and will have to fly into exile. That sounds terrible, one of his assistants points out. Su excelencia sir president I don't think women in this country are interested in politics, another assistant says cautiously, because he doesn't want to contradict the president. You are wrong, there are women involved in politics and they are dangerous... they are even worse than the men, the oldest member of the junta sighs, today, any woman could be a subversive, God knows what she could be! Mierda, sir president states, any woman! even your mother, wife, sister, maid, secretary, mother-in-law, daughter, granddaughter could be your traitor. Even the nuns who are our daughters' teachers. Even the prostitutes we bring for the soldiers. Mierda, that's true, the rest of the high command says, reaching the peak of realization. And don't forget, my Latin-American fellows, that justice is a woman holding a sword in one hand and a scale in the other, a U.S. general attending the meeting recalls, because he has just been given a golden statue of Justice as a gift for his 15 years of service in the government of su excelencia sir president. The president of the committee in charge of preparing the interrogation arrives and says, sir generals we are unable to do your assignment because we don't have enough information from you... Su excelencia sir president interrupts him and orders the members of the committee to commit suicide, otherwise they will be tortured to death under the charge of incompetence. The meeting ends with the problem unresolved.

This story also ends with the plot unresolved. However, history has shown us that the president's nightmare could come true, and in fact has been coming true...here and there and beyond, in big and small ways...

1981

? Or Else

There was a park. Or not. It was not a park. It might have been a small square. It had a few benches. It had some bushes and a couple of tall trees. It had a small statue of somebody.

It wasn't easy to find, or to see. Or to see it was a small square. (I am calling it "small square" but I am not sure what it was.)

There was a young woman entering the small square and sitting on a bench. I saw her from the sidewalk, right along the square.

She was wearing jeans, a blue shirt, a light blue handkerchief on her neck, a black beret and red tennis shoes. She had a notepad and a pen in her hand.

I decided to look at her without being noticed. A bush near the sidewalk helped me hide, a bit.

She looked at the sky, and wrote something. She looked at the ground, and wrote something. She looked at the trees, and wrote something. She looked in my direction and saw me, and wrote something.

Her notebook was small. Or that's what I thought. Where is she going to write when she finishes the pages of her small notebook? (This is a diversion/not my business/not my intention.)

She didn't raise her head for a while. She was writing and writing. And continued writing. She uncrossed her legs which she had crossed earlier. She continued writing.

She can't be writing, I thought, her notebook doesn't have any pages left, I thought. And she continued writing.

It has been more than three hours now, and she continues writing. I said to myself, I have been standing here for more than three hours too!

It's getting dark, I realized. And she continues writing, I saw.

I made a decision: I will approach her. (This is a diversion/not my business/not my intention, but I will approach her.)

I walked towards her. When I was close to her, she raised her head.

I was not surprised to see she was me. The red tennis shoes misled me a bit. Otherwise, I thought I had known all the time, over three hours now, that she was me.

There was a small square... (? Or else)

2021

MM en el P de la E

Había una mujer mala en el patio de la escuela. Nosotros la espiamos y cerramos bien la puerta del aula. También decidimos no salir al patio y no decir nada a la maestra que estaba por llegar de un momento a otro. La mujer mala en el patio de la escuela (MM en el P de la E) estaba sentada en una silla justo cerca del mástil del cual yo tendría que arriar la bandera dentro de unas horas. Dijimos que yo no iba a arriar la bandera dentro de unas horas porque si la MM en el P de la E me veía, me mataría. Había matado muchos chicos, y grandes también. Dicen que iba por detrás y los pinchaba con un alfiler o les cortaba la cabeza. Yo no quería estar sin cabeza, muy doloroso, y la maestra no llegaba no llegaba. Pancho pensó y dijo que a lo mejor la MM en el P de la E la había pinchado, pobre señorita, ella es grandota pero la otra es más grande. Pancho agregó que a lo mejor cuando tuvo que cruzar el patio para venir al aula, la MM en el P de la E la vio y fue por detrás a matarla. Y mientras hacíamos conjeturas sobre la maestra, espiábamos por el ojo de la cerradura para ver qué seguía haciendo la MM en el P de la E. Ella no seguía haciendo nada. Estaba sentada con la cabeza gacha el pelo rubio cayéndole en la cara las piernas extendidas los brazos caídos. Llevaba pantalones y una blusa y estaba descalza. "Yo sabía que vendría" no se cansaba de decir Anita "yo soñé anoche que vendría". Nuestra pregunta era "¿y qué le pasó a la maestra?" pero Anita tan misteriosa como siempre decía dándonos la espalda "qué sé yo hasta ahí no llegó mi sueño". Nos quedamos callados espiando por turno a la MM en la P de la E. La maestra no llegaba y suponíamos que ya era hora de salir y volver a casa. Beto propuso que como yo tenía que arriar la bandera, saliera antes de que sonara el timbre de salida y le hablara a la MM en el P de la E. Debía decirle que nosotros éramos buenos y no queríamos morir. Que por favor nos perdonara todas las acciones y omisiones malas y nos dejara ir a casa. Yo salí entonces con un miedo terrible y me acerqué lentamente a la MM en el P de la E. Cuando estaba a un metro de ella, le dije en voz baja "señora" y levantó la cabeza se quitó el pelo de la cara con las manos y descubrió ante mí –una de los veintidós alumnos de 3ro. - descubrió ante mí su rostro. Volví al aula corriendo y dije a todos que podíamos irnos. "¿Y la bandera?" me preguntaron. "Podemos irnos –vámonos" les dije "ella se encargará de la bandera". Salimos apretándonos contra la pared de las aulas, sin pasar por el medio del patio sin mirar a la silla ni al mástil ni a los brazos ni a los pies. Nos prometimos no decir nada a nadie y soportar cualquier castigo del director de la escuela por habernos ido antes. Decidimos pedir otra maestra y no comentar lo ocurrido a los chicos de los otros grados que indudablemente no la habían visto.

Al día siguiente el director nos retó. La maestra lloró de los nervios por el peligro que significó que escapáramos de la escuela. Ella había avisado que no podía asistir ese día y la dirección había llamado a una suplente que dijo que venía pero no se presentó. Todos tenían un poco de culpa en el incidente por lo tanto no nos amonestaron. El director me preguntó por qué había arriado y guardado la bandera en el armario. "Esa era mi tarea, señor director". Y volvimos al aula. La maestra nos esperaba con los números cuadrados en el pizarrón. Nos sonrió aliviada y todos le devolvimos la sonrisa. Nunca más volvimos a ver a la MM en el P de la E. Nunca más creo yo.

1985

"MM en el P de la E"

There was a bad woman in the schoolyard. We spied on her and then shut the classroom door tight. We also decided not to go out to the schoolyard and not say anything to the teacher who was about to arrive at any moment. The bad woman in the schoolyard (MM en el P de la E)[1] was sitting on a chair right near the flagpole from which I would have to lower the flag in a few hours. We said there was no way I was going to lower the flag in a few hours, because if the MM en el P de la E saw me, she would kill me. She had killed many children, and adults too. They say that she went from behind and pricked them with a pin or cut off their heads. I didn't want to be without a head, too painful, and the teacher didn't arrive didn't arrive. Pancho thought and said that maybe the MM en el P de la E had pricked her, poor señorita, she is big but the other is bigger. Pancho added that maybe when she had to cross the schoolyard to come to our classroom, the MM en el P de la E saw her and went from behind to kill her. And while we were guessing about

---

[1] The title of this story is an abbreviation for "mujer mala en el patio de la escuela" or "bad woman in the schoolyard."

the teacher, we peeped through the keyhole to see what the MM en el P de la E kept doing. She kept doing nothing. She was sitting bent over with her head down her light brown hair covering her face her legs out her arms collapsed at her side. She was wearing pants and a blouse and was barefoot. "I knew she would come" Anita never tired of saying, "I dreamt last night that she would come." Our question was "what happened to our teacher?" but Anita, mysterious as always, said turning her back to us "What do I know. My dream didn't get there." We stayed silent taking turns to spy on the MM en el P de la E. Our teacher did not arrive and we assumed that it was time to leave and go home. Beto suggested that since I had to lower the flag, I should go out of the classroom before the exit bell rang and talk to the MM en el P de la E. I had to tell her that we were good and we didn't want to die. To please forgive us all bad actions and omissions and let us go home. I went out with a terrible fear and slowly approached the MM en el P de la E. When I was a meter from her, I said to her in a low voice "ma'am" and she raised her head brushed her hair off her face with her hands and revealed to me – one of the twenty-two 3rd graders – revealed to me her face. I ran back to the classroom and told everybody that we could leave. "And the flag?" they asked me. "We can leave – let's go" I said "she will take care of the flag". We left pressing ourselves against the wall of the classrooms, without going to the middle of the schoolyard without looking at the chair or the flagpole or the arms or the feet. We promised ourselves not to say anything to anybody and to take any punishment from the school principal for leaving early. We decided to ask for another teacher and not comment on what had happened to the children in the other grades who undoubtedly had not seen her.

The next day the principal reprimanded us. Our teacher cried nervously because we had escaped from school and that was dangerous. She had said that she couldn't attend that day and the principal had called a substitute who said she was coming but didn't show up. They all had a little bit of blame in this incident therefore they did not send a note to our parents scolding us. The principal asked me why I had lowered the flag and put it away in the cabinet. "That's my task, sir." We went back to our classroom. The teacher was waiting for us with the square numbers on the blackboard. She smiled at us relieved and we all returned her smile. We never again saw the MM en el P de la E. Never again I believe.

2022

I Saw Her at the Corner of Page and Folsom
Waiting for the Bus

I saw her at the corner of Page and Folsom waiting for the bus. I was also waiting for the bus but going in the opposite direction. I crossed the street and greeted her casually as if it were yesterday. "Mari, I haven't seen you for a long time!" She looked at me and answered with the same tone of it-was-just-yesterday, "yes, it has been almost twenty-eight years." I continued showing surprise, "are you living in San Francisco now?" She was surrounded by young men and women who, I thought, naively, were her students. "Yes, I live in San Francisco. We moved here nineteen years ago." That is, I thought, in 1983. Where had she been between the time I had last seen her and '83? I recapitulated quickly: I saw her in '74, maybe April or May. '74. '73. '72. '72... She had a boyfriend who gave us the chills. "Us" meaning Cristina and me, who lived in the room next to where Mari and her roommate Amanda lived. (Two rooms on the roof, rented cheaply, on Belgrano Street.) Her boyfriend was a cop. Not any cop, he was a plainclothes cop. Times were difficult, and were becoming more difficult. Those were not times to be hanging around with the police.

Mari told me her boyfriend wanted to meet me, and take us out for dinner. She and I, with him out for dinner. I talked to Cristina: I couldn't say "no" because it would look suspicious. I could say "yes" and be extremely cautious in what I said. He already knew Cristina and I were students at the Facultad de Humanidades, that "hotbed of radical leftists."

"Where are you going with your students?" I said, aware that Mari hadn't even gone to high school when I knew her. "They are not my students," she replied smiling, "they are my sons and daughters. These are my children. Well, grown-up now". I quickly thought of my next question which I didn't ask, "adopted children?" They looked all different in size and color but most of them seemed to be about the same age, around 20ish. I couldn't ask her about their age: the bus had just arrived and I felt embarrassed by my former question: she knew that I knew she had never studied beyond elementary school, so what was the point in asking if they were her students.

Her boyfriend came to get us and the three of us walked downtown, seven or eight blocks from where we lived. The first stop was in this old, big café-restaurant I passed by every day on my way to work but I had never tried before, eloquently called Palacio Royal. We sat in a booth and had copas Melba. We chatted about nothing in particular until Mari spilt some of her copa on her boyfriend's suit. We laughed, I cautiously, like everything else I did that evening. He didn't like it of course, but kept his composure.

As "her children" were getting on the bus I asked her what had made her decide to come to the U.S. and San Francisco in particular. "We had too many children, we couldn't stay."

The next stop was at another café-restaurant of which I don't remember the name or much else except for the efficient young waitress. We sat at a table on the sidewalk. It was hot: December, always hot and humid. He wanted to talk about the Facultad where I studied. I was trying to play the role of dumb and naïve. A role hard to believe for somebody who knew "there were no innocents at the Facultad de Humanidades." Mari made some jokes, I laughed stupidly, and he kept looking at me.

"Her children" were still getting on the bus. I didn't count how many there were. I regret it now, because knowing exactly how many sons and daughters she had would have given me some certainty. I remained standing there, wanting to ask her more and more questions. Finally, "are you married?" – a question I never ask. In retrospect, I see that my intuition was directing me towards a resolution I was expecting and at the same time didn't want to know. She smiled for an answer, and then said, "I told you "we" came to the US." I insisted, "you came with all your sons and daughters, right?" Smiled again.

He kept looking at me, and said, "we arrested several activists yesterday." Mari asked him how they had done it. He said, not looking at me but smiling, "some smart interrogation."

Mari looked at me intensely and said, "my husband came too. We all came to the US." We didn't have more time. She was getting on the bus, now full with her sons and daughters. She turned to me for one last comment, "you remember Juan, my boyfriend, don't you? The three of us went out for dinner in December '72. Juan and I adopted many children several years after we got married. We couldn't have any, so we adopted. Orphaned babies need a home too, and we love children." We waved our hands and said good-bye. The door closed, and the bus left. I thought, "I take that bus often: it's the line that passes close to my work." I crossed the street and went back to the bus stop where I was before all this started. As I got on my bus, I wasn't sure if I had had a dream or if this was one of the many tricks Time plays when I think I am seeing somebody from my past. That's why it would have been helpful to know exactly how many sons and daughters she had. But, who knows, I could have been, in any case, building a certainty from a dream.

2022

Little Annie

I had walked several blocks from the park when this friend crossing the street yelled at me, "hey, you lost the child!" I looked down at the stroller and Annie wasn't there. "Shit!", I said, "how could I lose Annie?!" I rushed back the way I had come. Obviously Annie had leaned on one side and had fallen out of the stroller. I arrived back in the park. "Annie, Annie, where are you!", I first murmured, then said aloud. "Her mother is going to kill me," I thought. I had just started to babysit for her. It was my only job at the moment. I wanted to prove I was careful and caring and sensitive and etc, etc. "She will kill me and will never recommend me to anybody... or first the latter and second the former." "Annie, where are you?!," I asked again. "Are you looking for that child?," an older woman who was feeding the pigeons asked me. "Yes!", I said in desperation. "No, not that one!", I added disappointed and almost in panic as I saw that child's mother picking him up and walking away. "Then, maybe this one with a pigeon in her hand?" "Yes! Annie, dear, what happened? I am sorry." Annie didn't seem to care much. She was mumbling something to the pigeon. I said, "tell the pigeon good bye and let's go back home." I picked her up, kissed her and sat her in the stroller. We headed back home. The pigeon followed us. I asked Annie to tell the pigeon to go back to the park and we will go back the next afternoon. Annie smiled at me, and then mumbled something to the pigeon. She continued following us. We arrived home, I lifted Annie from the stroller and left her on the ground while I opened the door. The pigeon was still with us. We went inside, and the pigeon came too. "Annie, we can't have her in the house! Your mother is going to fire me!" Annie smiled, her sweet smile as always, and didn't say anything. The two of them walked into Annie's room. I tried to get the pigeon but Annie closed the door in my face. I thought, "well, so much for my babysitter job." I sat on a sofa waiting for Annie to open the door, or worse, for her mother to come back home. Annie did open the door after a while, and the two of them came out of the room. I saw Annie climbing a chair and opening one of the windows. The pigeon climbed to the windowsill, looked at Annie (I swear they smiled at each other), and flew away. I looked at her and smiled too. "Tomorrow my friend will be in the park again," she said. "Of course, Annie, tomorrow and the day after tomorrow, at 2pm in the park, in this beautiful spring that brings your friend the pigeon. What did the two of you talk about, Annie?"

1993-2016

Ute, the Silver Tabby Cat

In her honor

There was a silver tabby cat, Ute, who lived with her moms in a house with a garden. She loved to go to the garden every day, even when it was raining. She loved to sit there and look at the butterflies, blue jays and hummingbirds who visited the garden almost every day. She liked to sit in the sun, or if it was hot, in the shade. Her moms went with her to the garden, or they kept an eye on her if they were inside the house. Ute also enjoyed being in the house, sitting on one of her mom's desk or sitting on one of her scratching posts to look outside, to the garden or to the street. She enjoyed most of all sitting on her scratching post in the living room looking to the east when the sun was rising. Ute marveled at the sunrise. As she also marveled at the first drops of rain, trying to catch them through the window.

Ute and her two moms were happy living together. There were many moments when her moms seemed to have problems or sorrows. Ute took care of them very lovingly and patiently. Ute herself had several illnesses and had to be treated, even twice she had surgery, and she didn't like that. She preferred not to remember those moments.

As always happens, time passed, and kept passing. Days and nights, seasons and full moons, storms with heavy rain and droughts. Everything was passing, and passed.

Ute and her moms lived a long life together. Ute was their friend, companion and teacher.

The three of them were getting older together. But Ute got sick, then very sick, then she passed away. She lived 19 years, 3 months and 12 and a half days.

....

The women sat in their garden, where they used to sit with their Ute. They did so every morning and then again in the late afternoon. It was the beginning of Autumn, and the sun in the garden was warm and cozy. The leaves were falling from the laurel tree in the neighbor's backyard and were covering a stretch of their garden. The lemon tree, near where they sat, was full of lemons: generous and prolific tree it was.

There were birds and butterflies who came and went, and flew around in the garden. Ute used to love them, and the women loved them too.

One day, in the middle of Autumn, in the late afternoon, a blue jay came and stayed next to these women who were sitting on one of the stones. The women looked at her. The blue jay looked at them. The three of them stayed together in silence for a long time.

Then, the blue jay flew away.

The next day, in the late afternoon, the blue jay came back and stayed with the women. The three of them in silence, keeping each other company.

Then, the blue jay flew away.

Again, two days later, in the late afternoon, the blue jay came back and stayed with them, sitting on a stone in their garden. The women were crying.

Then, the blue jay sat on one of their shoulders. They stopped crying and smiled. The first time they had smiled in a long time.

After a long while, the blue jay left.

Time passed, the women were still very much missing their cat Ute, and now they were missing the blue jay: she hadn't shown up lately.

But then, they saw a bee pollinating a flower in the lemon tree. Bees came to the lemon tree, but they hadn't paid attention to them.

The bee looked at the women, came very close to them, and sat on the stone too.

They stayed together for a long time, almost until dark. The women felt the bee's company, and smiled.

Two days later, again, the women and the bee sat on the stone in the garden. In silence, they kept each other company.

And, as always happens, time passed. And time kept passing.

The women came every day to the garden and sat there. But the blue jay didn't come back and the bee didn't either.

Until one day, they went out of their house. They walk outside next to their house: there was an open space there, with plants and flowers. They saw the blue jay, and they saw the bee!

Hi friends, they said to them.

The blue jay flew very close to them, and the bee stopped pollinating a California poppy and flew very close to them too.

They both took the women farther down into this open space. They took them to…

Who was down there? Sitting on the grass?

A silver tabby cat was sitting on the grass!

The women looked at her. The cat looked at the women. The blue jay and the bee seemed to try to say something. They kept flying around the women and the cat.

Then, the women understood. They understood and smiled.

The silver tabby cat got up.

One of the women lifted her, and put her against her chest. The cat rubbed her head against the woman's chest.

They said thank you to the blue jay and thank you to the bee, and walked back home carrying their new silver tabby cat.

As they were opening the front door, one of them said to the cat: we will give you some food and water now. We will discuss your name later.

They lived happily together going to the garden in the morning and afternoon, and sitting on the stone. The women smiled every day, many times. The cat rubbed her head against the women's bodies every day, many times.

This is the story of a noble and loving silver tabby cat who couldn't bear seeing her moms so sad and crying, and decided to come back herself or send a sister cat, so her moms wouldn't be sad and crying, but happy and smiling.

And that's exactly what happened. You can still see them together in the garden or inside their home. In the Autumn and in the Spring. And with everything fulfilling the cycle of Life.

2019

Atardecer/anochecer – un dilema

Atardecer. Anochecer. ¡Qué línea tan sutil separa uno del otro! Una línea invisible. De éso me dí cuenta hace mucho tiempo: una línea invisible. Traté de mirar fijamente el atardecer para reconocer el momento exacto cuando se convierte en anochecer. Imposible: la línea es invisible. O, en términos de tiempo: el momento es imperceptible. Entonces decidí vivir haciendo un esfuerzo para no prestar atención al cambio, ese cambio tan sutil e imperceptible, ese momento que dura 3 segundos o no sé. A pesar de que era consciente de que estaba ignorando un cambio profundo y trascendental. A pesar de que todos los días a eso del atardecer/anochecer me mordía los labios para no preguntar, enterraba la incertidumbre para no pensar. A veces no podía resistir y decía a mis amigos/as: "qué hermoso atardecer". Frase tan cotidiana que no debería traer consecuencias o causar alarma. Sin embargo, no faltaba alguien que dijera: "anochecer, dirás". Un día ellos/ellas, mis amigos y amigas, trajeron el tema a la mesa del café, sin saber ni por asomo de mi solitaria lucha por alejar el interrogante. Ernesto dijo: "el atardecer ocurre cuando el sol se ha puesto". "No necesariamente", contestó Isabel, que había estudiado los fenómenos físicos por más de quince años. "No vale la pena preocuparse hoy justamente, dado que está lloviendo…", agregó Jorge, conciliatorio. Pero, para Isabel, que había estudiado los fenómenos físicos por más de quince años, la discusión sobre este tema era un asunto serio que no podía dejarse, como a veces abandonábamos discusiones sobre el último submarino visto en la costa, el mejor medio de transporte para mudar casas, la extinción de tiburones y su impacto sobre la industria cinematográfica de Hollywood o las últimas y las próximas elecciones presidenciales. "Es una discusión seria, el atardecer y el anochecer", dijo Isabel. Yo sufría. No hablaba. Hasta que alguien recordó mi comentario "qué hermoso atardecer" y las miradas cayeron sobre mí, pesadas, con la pregunta: "¿vos, que pensás?". No quise responder: "no pienso nada", porque sabía que Ernesto iba a decir: "siempre pensamos algo", entonces dije que no lo tenía resuelto, que necesitaba leer sobre el tema pero no había tenido tiempo de hacerlo. Y recalqué: "no tuve tiempo", queriendo evitar el reproche de Isabel. Ella me miró, me perdonó y continuó. Pero sus explicaciones y argumentos no echaron luz sobre mi ceguera: todavía no pude ver la línea sutil que separa el atardecer del anochecer. Jorge concluyó, para poder irse: "no es sólo una cuestión física, es tambien filosófica". Aprovechando que él se levantaba, me levanté también diciendo: "tengo que volver a casa, me olvidé de dar de comer a la gata". Por supuesto, ellos/ellas piensan que mi gata puede esperar, pero también saben que yo pienso que mi gata no puede esperar, entonces no hubo ni comentarios ni críticas, sólo un saludo cordial e Isabel diciéndome que iba a prestarme un libro sobre el tema.

"No, no!", le dije a mi gata mientras le ponía pedacitos de hígado en su plato, "no quiero pensar en éso, he decidido vivir sin pensar en éso". Ella me miró, más bien contrariada por la tardanza de su comida, y en sus ojos dorados, grandes y profundos leí lo que me había imaginado: mi gata había dejado de preocuparse por el atardecer/anochecer hacía mucho tiempo y por eso era felíz. Una vez más me propuse no preocuparme. "Seguí el ejemplo de tu gata", me dije. Pero, a diferencia de ella, he necesitado asistir a varias secciones de meditación trascendental y todavía voy a un psicólogo que me ayuda en el arte de no pensar en el atardecer/anochecer.

1989

Sunset/Twilight: A Dilemma

Sunset. Twilight. What a subtle line separates one from the other! An invisible line. I realized this a long time ago: an invisible line. I tried to stare at the sunset to recognize the exact moment when it becomes twilight. Impossible: the line is invisible. Or, in terms of time: the moment is imperceptible. Then, I decided to live making an effort not to pay attention to the change, that subtle and imperceptible change, that moment that lasts three seconds or I don't know. Despite I was aware that I was ignoring a profound and transcendental change. Despite that every day around the time of sunset/twilight I bit my lips not to ask, I buried the uncertainty so as not to think. Sometimes, I couldn't resist and I told my friends: "what a beautiful sunset". A phrase so everyday that it shouldn't bring consequences or cause alarm. However, there was never a lack of someone who said, "Twilight, you should say". One day, they, my friends, brought the subject to the café table, not knowing anything about my lonely struggle to push the question away. Ernesto said, "sunset happens after the sun has set." "Not necessarily," answered Isabel, who had studied physical phenomena for more than fifteen years. "It's not worth worrying about it today exactly, if it's raining…," added Jorge, conciliatory. But, for Isabel, who had studied physical phenomena for more than fifteen years, it was a serious discussion that could not be left alone, like sometimes the discussions we abandoned about the last submarine seen near the coast, the best means of transport to move houses, the extinction of sharks and its impact on the Hollywood film industry, or the last and next presidential elections. "This is a serious subject, the sunset and the twilight", remarked Isabel. I was suffering. I didn't talk. Until someone remembered my comment "what a beautiful sunset" and the eyes fell on me, heavy, with the question, "what do you think?" I didn't want to answer, "I don't think anything", because I knew Ernesto would say, "That's not true, we always think something", so I said that I hadn't solved it, that I needed to read about it but hadn't had the time. And I emphasized, "I did not have time", wanting to avoid Isabel's reproach. She looked at me, forgave me and continued. But her explanations and arguments did not shed light on my blindness: I still could not see the subtle line that separates sunset from twilight. So as to be able to leave, Jorge concluded, "it is not only a physical question, it is also a philosophical one." Taking advantage of the fact that he was getting up, I also got up saying, "I have to go home, I forgot to feed my cat." Of course, they think my cat can wait, but they also know that I think my cat cannot wait, so there were no comments or criticisms, just a friendly goodbye and Isabel telling me she was going to lend me a book on the subject.

"No, no!", I told my cat while I was putting little pieces of liver in her bowl, "I don't want to think about it, I have decided to live without thinking about it." She looked at me, rather annoyed about the delay in giving her food, and in her golden eyes, big and deep, I read what I had imagined: my cat had stopped worrying about sunset/twilight a long time ago and that's why she's happy. "Follow your cat's example", I told myself. But, unlike her, I have needed to attend several sessions of transcendental meditation, and I still go to a psychologist who helps me in the art of not thinking about sunset/twilight.

2022

Canción infantil de ayer

– con variaciones necesarias de hoy

A todas las lobas y lobitas. A todos los lobos y lobitos

Juguemos en el bosque/mientras la loba no está/loba está?

Me estoy poniendo los pantalones

Juguemos en el bosque/mientras la loba no está/loba está?

Me estoy poniendo la camiseta

Juguemos en el bosque/mientras la loba no está/loba está?

Me estoy poniendo la camisa

Juguemos en el bosque/mientas la loba no está/loba está?

Me estoy poniendo las medias

Juguemos en el bosque/mientras la loba no está/loba está?

Me estoy poniendo las zapatillas

Juguemos en el bosque/mientras la loba no está/loba está?

Estoy cerrando la puerta y salgo

Juguemos en el bosque/mientras la loba no está/loba está?

……………………..

Juguemos en el bosque/mientras la loba no está/loba está?

……………………..

Juguemos en el bosque/mientras la loba no está/loba está?

……………………..

Loba está? – Loba estás? – Dónde estás? – Así no vale:

¡Queremos jugar con vos!

¡Como lo hicimos ayer, anteayer, y anteayer!

……………………..

Niños: ya lo agarramos y lo matamos. ¡Están a salvo de ese animal! Vayan a su casa. Vayan a la cama. Crezcan sanos. Mañana será otro día, sin animales crueles y voraces.

Pero señor: ¡queríamos jugar con la loba! ¡Hace mucho que jugamos con ella!

……………………

Juguemos en el bosque/mientras los hombres no están/hombres están?

Aquí estoy, aquí estamos. Vayan a la cama. Mañana será otro día, y ustedes tienen que crecer.

………………….

Juguemos en el bosque………… Jugábamos en el bosque con la loba/mientras el hombre no estaba.

Pero ya no hay loba ni bosque.

Y hemos crecido, con una lobita en nuestros corazones.

2022

Children's Spanish Round from the Past – With Some Necessary Variations from Today

To the wolves, small and big, young and old

Let's play in the woods/ while the wolf is not here/Wolf, are you here?

I am putting my pants on

Let's play in the woods/ while the wolf is not here/Wolf, are you here?

I am putting my shirt on

Let's play in the woods/ while the wolf is not here/Wolf, are you here?

I am putting my socks on

Let's play in the woods/ while the wolf is not here/Wolf, are you here?

I am putting my shoes on

Let's play in the woods/ while the wolf is not here/Wolf, are you here?

I am closing the door and going out

Let's play in the woods/ while the wolf is not here/Wolf, are you here?

....

Let's play in the woods/ while the wolf is not here/Wolf, are you here?

....

Let's play in the woods/while the wolf is not here/Wolf, are you here?

....

Is the wolf here? – Wolf, are you here? – Where are you? – That's not okay:

We want to play with you!

Like we did yesterday, and the day before yesterday, and the day before that!

....

That's it, children! We caught it and killed it. You are saved from that animal! You can go home, go to bed, and grow up healthy. Tomorrow will be another day, without cruel and voracious animals.

But sir: we wanted to play with her! We have been playing with her for a long time!

....

Let's play in the woods while the men are not here! Men, are you here?

Here I am, here we are. Go to bed. Tomorrow will be another day, and you have to grow up.

....

Let's play in the woods .... We played in the woods with the wolf/ while man was not there.

But there is no wolf or woods anymore.

And we have grown up, with a little wolf in our hearts.

2022

Intermezzo

Agarró sus poemas y salió a la calle. Una tarde de lluvia salió a la calle con sus poemas a cantarlos. A cantarlos y gritarlos, si era necesario. A golpear de puerta en puerta como una Testigo de la Poesía diciendo buenas tardes señora buenas tardes señor aquí traigo la llave de su salvación. Léalos, piénselos, ámelos, cántelos, siga en pos de ellos que le iluminarán su camino. Aprenda estos nombres Lorde, Rimbaud, Vallejo, Peri Rossi, Machado, Celan, Castellanos, Safo... y muchas/os más. Aprenda los nombres de las discípulas y los discípulos. Búsquelas y búsquelos en la jornada de cada día. Ponga guirnaldas de balcón a balcón de ventana a ventana de estrella a estrella y baile. Baile. Celebre el advenimiento de la salvadora. Aquí se la traigo. Ahora es suya. Golpeando en cada puerta, gritando, cantando, bailando, una tarde de lluvia salió a la calle. Con sus poemas con sus poemas. Y cuando una niña la escuchó, vino un coche con luces rojas y un hombre vestido de policía se llevó a la Testigo porque –le dijo- aquí hay muchos salvadores y ya todo está bien. No necesitamos más nada. Y la niña corrió con los poemas y los guardó bajo la almohada, para sacarlos otro día de lluvia y una noche de estrellas. Así por siempre y para siempre.

1994

Intermezzo

She took her poems and went to the street. On a rainy
afternoon she went out with her poems to sing them. To sing
them, and shout them, if necessary. Knocking from door to
door as a Witness of Poetry saying good afternoon madam
good afternoon sir here I bring the key to your salvation.
Read them, think about them, love them, sing them, follow
after them that they will light your way. Learn these names
Lorde, Rimbaud, Vallejo, Peri Rossi, Machado, Celan,
Castellanos, Sappho… and many more. Learn the names of
their disciples. Look for them each day. Put garlands from
balcony to balcony from window to window from star to star
and dance. Dance. Celebrate the advent of the savior. I bring
it here to you. Now it is yours. Knocking from door to door,
shouting, singing, dancing, on a rainy afternoon she went to
the street. With her poems, with her poems. And just when a
girl heard her, a car with red lights arrived and a man
dressed as the police took the Witness because – he said-
there are many saviors here and everything is already fine.
We don't need anything else. And the girl ran with the
poems and kept them under her pillow, to take them out on

another day of rain and in a night of stars. Like that forever
and ever.

2022

An Occasional Meeting

The man who had fallen in love with the Autumn met the woman who had been more than a hundred years in the tin box's label of an India and Ceylon blend tea. Whether this encounter had been planned, materially and/or mentally, we will never know. Maybe it was An Occasional Meeting, as the title suggests.

Sort of unusual, the encounter I mean, considering they came from such different backgrounds, countries, cultures, languages and, naturally, personal histories.

Our man who had fallen in love with Autumn came from a small town in the southern hemisphere where they spoke Spanish (that's why his story is originally titled, *Un hombre/el otoño*). His love started when he was a child: during the siesta time, he would go to the outskirts of the town to walk in solitude. There he saw and fell for Autumn. Very deeply. So profoundly that it completely changed his life. When he grew up he decided to follow Autumn everywhere it was, wherever it was going. A lot of traveling, I would say. But that was the man who fell for Autumn. Dry leaves, orange voices from the kitchen, clothes tended in lines drying outside in backyards or near lakes and rivers, men chatting outside their front door or in the plaza. Migration of birds, singing songs as they flew towards the Spring or towards the Fall, learning different national anthems in their original languages as they flew over different countries. Our man with a small suitcase and a notebook, trying not to call much attention, but talking to people and asking them about their Autumn. Only a young girl apparently understood what he was doing, because she told him that she, too, was in love with Autumn.

The woman who had lived for over one hundred years in the tin tea box's label, small tin box's label, came from an immense house with an immense garden in a city in the northern hemisphere where they spoke English (that's why her (sort of) story is originally titled, *Looking for Safety*, referring to the narrator of the story, and not to the woman who in fact was a second character in it). She loved her security and being so protected by her family, her days spent drinking tea and reading poetry. But it seems that so many years of safety, tea, protection and poetry produced dissatisfaction in her that turned into deep boredom. That was when, taking advantage of the narrator of the story's fear, she asked her to change places and went off to see the world. Her travels were many and confusing at the beginning, so disoriented she was in a different time and so many different places. How can the world be so vast and diverse? How can time have passed so quickly and inexorably? It took her, yes, time, to adjust to new environments and times. She missed her teas and poetry and the garden and the protection, until she realized she could still have some tea, poetry, plants, flowers and birds, if not her family's protection and her fiancé's poems.

The woman (for abbreviation let's call her "woman/100 years/tin box label") had heard there was very good tea and poetry in a city by a bay, and she very badly wanted to have specifically the blend of India and Ceylon tea. (To add to her many confusions, somebody told her that Ceylon was not Ceylon anymore it was called Sri Lanka.) She was also missing poetry: the romantic, languishing poetry of her fiancé and others. (To add to her many confusions, somebody sent her to a bookstore with a lot of poetry, but not so languishing, not so romantic as she had been exposed to.)

Their encounter, supposedly by chance (or not), was difficult and frustrating. Different languages, different cultures, different pursuits in life. We don't know what the woman/100 years/tin box label was pursuing in life but it seems certain it was not Autumn. The man/ Autumn was very clear about his passion, but didn't want to reveal it to her, not right away in any case. They enjoyed sipping tea in silence for a couple of hours until he suggested they walk around the city. He wanted his new friend to see Autumn in this city, but he was having trouble to see and to hear the orange voices from a kitchen, the immensity of brown leaves on the ground, the clothes drying outside in yards or near the bay...

After walking for several hours, they both realized they didn't have much to talk about or to share. She kept talking about what she knew, sitting in her room, looking at her immense garden and more tea and more tea, but no poems. He kept talking about what he knew, Autumn and how Autumn was telling him stories he wanted to write down and not forget. When she talked, he looked at her in confusion and disbelief. When he talked, she looked at him in confusion and disbelief.

Until they heard a voice, a female voice, calling on her from a distant past and place, asking her to please come back. The voice or the woman with that voice was tired and bored with so much tea, garden, poems which she couldn't relate to, flying onto the small table and piling up there waiting to be read. She was not looking for safety any longer, she said. She wanted to come back to her place and time. Please, *you* come back to your room, there is plenty of tea and there will be for many years!

So the woman/100 years/tin box label decided to go back. It's my destiny, she thought. Maybe I can make some changes, she thought, less tea, better poems, no fiancé. What am I saying? No fiancé! That's going to be hard. Let's see...

The man/Autumn was eager to be able to continue his incessant passion, his endless pursuit. He went back to his small town, but just for a while, to see Autumn, and left. He continues pursuing Autumn around the globe. You might see him in a town, on a hill, in a valley, in a forest, in a city, on a farm. Always following Autumn. Say hello to him, but do not interfere with his pursuit and his passion. He is in love.

As for the woman/100 years/tin box label, you might not see her in her family's immense estate. It's clear she made some big changes in her life. Don't be surprised if you happen to see her in another place and time marching and chanting in the streets with many people of different colors, ages, genders, backgrounds, abilities. She is in love.

2021

Exiting Remarks

Long time ago, 60 or 20 years ago, in some remote area of this planet,

Matilde, the cow, said approximately these words:
"When he was younger, Mark Twain would remember anything, whether it had happened or not."

Aurora, the parrot, said approximately these words:
"Remembering is sometimes like dreaming."

2022